CALLING the WATER DRUM

by **LaTisha Redding**

illustrated by **Aaron Boyd**

Lee & Low Books Inc. *New York*

LEE & LOW BOOKS INC., 95 Madison Avenue, New York, NY 10016
leeandlow.com
Book design by Christy Hale
Book production by The Kids at Our House
The text is set in Goudy Old Style
The illustrations are rendered in watercolor
Manufactured in China by Jade Productions, August 2016
Printed on paper from responsible sources
10 9 8 7 6 5 4 3 2 1
First Edition

Library of Congress Cataloging-in-Publication Data
Names: Redding, LaTisha, author. | Boyd, Aaron, 1971- illustrator.
Title: Calling the water drum / by LaTisha Redding ; illustrated by
Aaron Boyd.
Description: First edition. | New York, NY : Lee & Low Books Inc., 2016. |
    Summary: "A young boy loses both parents as they attempt to flee
Haiti for a better life, and afterward is only able to process his grief and
communicate with the outside world through playing the drums. Includes
author's note"— Provided by publisher.
Identifiers: LCCN 2015032606 | ISBN 9781620141946 (hardcover:
alk. paper)
Subjects: | CYAC: Drum—Fiction. | Selective mutism—Fiction. |
    Orphans—Fiction. | Immigrants—New York (State)—New York—
    Fiction. | Haitian Americans—Fiction. | New York (N.Y.)—Fiction.
Classification: LCC PZ7.1.R4 Cal 2016 | DDC [E]—dc23
LC record available at http://lccn.loc.gov/2015032606

For my parents, who cultivated my love of story—L.R.

For Sabri, the best—A.B.

Day after day I pound my drum. *Tat-tat-tat-tat.*

My friend, Karrine, asks, "Henri, why do you bang on that drum so?"

I don't answer. I close my eyes and strike my drum again, the rhythm pulsing from my heart through my hands.

Karrine and I are the same age. She looks as if she could be my *sè*, my sister. And some days it feels as if she is. Karrine lives with her mother in the apartment next door. They have known my uncle, Jacques, longer than me.

We live on a long street that is noisy all day and all night with many different sounds. Inside our apartment building, it is always cold and quiet. I don't like the quiet, and I thump that into my drum too.

My drum is really an old bucket. It is what I used to help Manman carry water when we lived in Haiti.

One day Uncle Jacques sent a letter asking us to leave Haiti and stay with him in New York. This made Manman and Papa very happy, and they hugged me many times. Uncle Jacques sent money too. We needed it to buy a boat to cross to the other side of the great water. Papa said not to tell anyone in our village about the letter and money.

Later, during our long walk to the market, Manman said that once we crossed the water I could go to school. This made me very happy.

We left Haiti in the middle of the night so no one would see us.
I wondered if our friends would miss us.

"You will make new friends," Manman told me.

We had only enough money to buy a rickety boat from a fisherman.
The boat was so old it let in some water. At first the boat rocked gently,
but then the waves were rough and the boat rocked harder and harder
as we moved away from the shore. We didn't know how to swim and
tried our best to hold on to the sides of the boat. I told my parents
I was *pè*, scared.

Manman put her arm around me and placed a finger on her lips,
telling me to be quiet. There was a much larger boat in the distance with
many lights. We paddled our boat away from it and into the darkness.

The water was calmer farther out at sea. I listened to the hum of Manman's and Papa's voices over the water. A warm wind touched my face. The salty water gently tapped against our boat and splashed up my arms. When Papa grew tired of paddling, we drifted for a while.

Manman showed me my uncle's letter again and then put it into my pocket. I fell asleep and dreamed about what our new life would be like. Would I like school? Would I make new friends?

During the night, the waves became
rough again, and our small boat rocked back and
forth. The boat started to fill up with water. Papa scooped
out the water with the bucket while Manman and I used our hands.

Our boat overturned. Papa put me on top of the boat and gave me
the bucket. Manman held on to the boat, and Papa held on to Manman.

The water swirled around my parents and pulled them away from the boat.
And from me. The waves pushed them farther and farther away until I could
not see them anymore.

All night I yelled, "Manman! Papa!" No one answered.

In the morning, I saw another small boat nearby. The people saw me and pulled me inside. They had just left Haiti too. They asked me my name, but I could not speak. Instead I looked for Manman and Papa in the foamy water. I saw nothing.

When we finally reached the shore, the boat people asked me my name again, but I still could not speak. I gave them the letter in my pocket that had my uncle's information. They sent for him in New York. I held on to my bucket.

Everyone talked around me and whispered about how I came to be alone in the water.

My uncle was kind to me, much like my papa. And he fed me rice and beans, like my manman. When I first came to stay, Karrine asked me many questions that I could not answer.

I had no words for anyone. Nothing in Creole and nothing in this English that my uncle tried to teach me.

So Karrine took my bucket and tapped its side. "One for 'yes,'" she said. "Two for 'no.'"

I liked the sound the bucket made. *Bang.* It called to me, and I tapped it more. *Bang. Bang.* Sometimes I filled it with water, searching for a different sound. **Doon-doon-doon.**

I took my bucket with me everywhere, even when we went out to play.
One day I picked up a branch and thumped the bucket—

Thwack . . . thwack! Thwack!

I couldn't stop hitting it until—*Crick*. The branch broke in my hand, and I flung it aside. I turned the bucket upside down and pounded it with my palms. A familiar sound came out. It was deep like Papa's voice and warm like Manman's laugh.

Every day I played my drum, pounding it until I was sweating. I got really good at drumming.

After school, my uncle took me to the park, and I sat with my drum. I didn't feel the frosty air as people gathered around and listened to me play.

Instead I listened for the sound of my manman and my papa.

Sometimes Karrine comes to hear me play, but she doesn't stay long. She doesn't like crowds of people. She lost her father after a hurricane in Louisiana, and crowds make her think about the time after the hurricane.

But today there are no crowds around, and Karrine says softly, "I miss my daddy, Henri. Do you miss your parents?"

I stop playing, and a sound rises like a wave in my throat. I open my mouth, and one word spills out. "*Wi.*" Yes.

Karrine sits next to me and taps on the bench. Karrine's mom is there too. She laughs as Uncle Jacques claps and dances to the beat. She joins in too. The sounds makes me happy.

I keep pounding my drum. I hope the rhythm pulsing from my heart through my hands reaches Manman and Papa, and Karrine's father too.

Author's note

I am from the South. When I was a child, my parents left the South with my siblings and me, and we moved to New York City. There we discovered that being Southern meant we were different. We spoke with accents and didn't sound like the other children in our new neighborhood.

Luckily, I quickly made friends with the kids in my elementary school. And to my surprise, some of my classmates had accents too and spoke other languages as well as English. I learned that they had arrived recently from other parts of the world: Haiti, Sweden, and Puerto Rico. I was surrounded by children whose families, like mine, had journeyed to New York for better opportunities. Later, other classmates were from Barbados, China, Germany, Jamaica, Russia, Trinidad, and Spain.

My friends and I exchanged stories often, and their stories have stayed with me. But the hushed stories some of my Haitian friends told of how they arrived in the United States were vastly different from the stories of other friends. It wasn't just the culture shock and feelings of not belonging that frightened them. The journey to the United States was dangerous, and this has not changed much in the decades since I first heard my friends' stories. According to US Coast Guard statistics, the greatest number of Haitians rescued at sea was more than 37,500 in 1992. The number in 2015 was still more than 400. These numbers do not include Haitians who were not rescued because they either drowned or made it safely to Florida's shores without being detected.

Haitians are not alone. People in many other parts of the world are crossing oceans in battered boats, and some are crossing deserts in scorching heat. They are holding tightly to a vision of life beyond mere survival for themselves.

It is these unsettling memories, images, and facts that spurred me to write this story. I want readers of *Calling the Water Drum* to know that I formed Henri's story to reflect both the uncertainty and the hope that exist side by side with sacrifice and courage in forging a new life.

source of statistics: United States Coast Guard:http://www.uscg.mil/hq/cg5/cg531/AMIO/FlowStats/FY.asp.